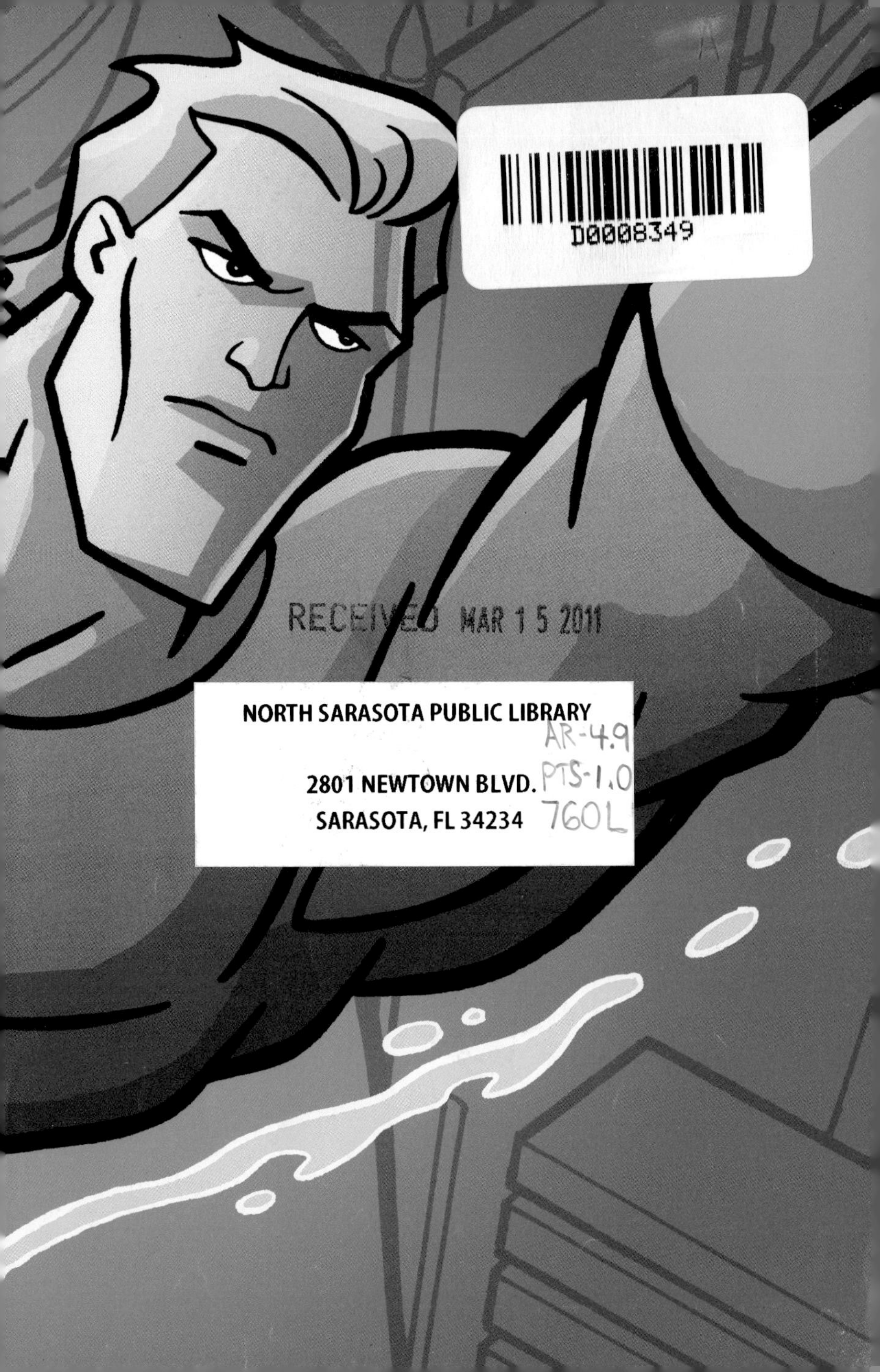

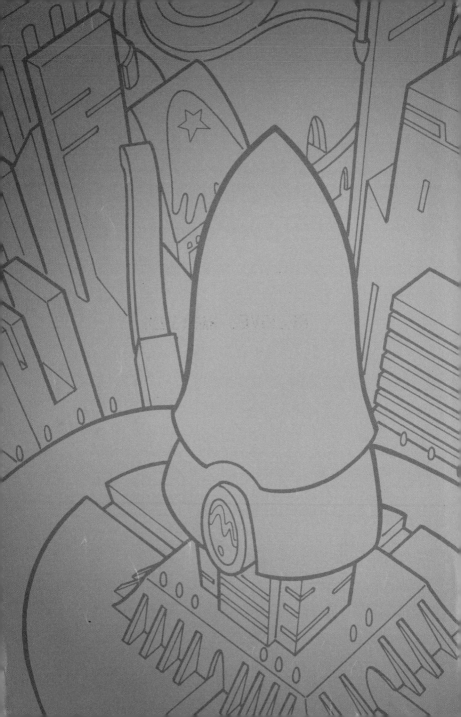

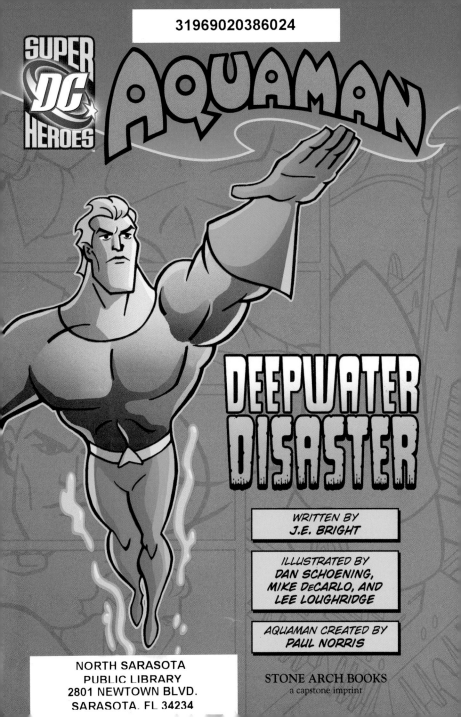

SUPER DC HEROES

AQUAMAN

DEEPWATER DISASTER

WRITTEN BY
J.E. BRIGHT

ILLUSTRATED BY
DAN SCHOENING,
MIKE DeCARLO, AND
LEE LOUGHRIDGE

AQUAMAN CREATED BY
PAUL NORRIS

STONE ARCH BOOKS
a capstone imprint

Published by Stone Arch Books in 2011
A Capstone Imprint
151 Good Counsel Drive, P.O. Box 669
Mankato, Minnesota 56002
www.capstonepub.com

Cataloging-in-Publication Data is available on the
Library of Congress website.

ISBN: 978-1-4342-3317-2 (library binding)

Summary: A violent storm strikes the Gulf of
Mexico, damaging a drilling rig off the Louisiana
coast. Only one man can stop millions of barrels of
oil from spilling into the ocean . . . Aquaman, the
King of the Sea! Without delay, the super hero and
his underwater friends surge toward the disaster.
Suddenly, out of a black plume of oil, an even greater
darkness emerges. The evil Black Manta is siphoning
oil into his submarine. The Sea King can't believe the
villain could sink to such terrible depths! Before the
gulf is destroyed, Aquaman must convince his enemy
that a threat to the sea is a threat to them both.

Art Director: Bob Lentz
Designer: Brann Garvey
Production Specialist: Michelle Biedscheid

Printed in the United States of America in Stevens Point, Wisconsin.
122010
006026WZS11

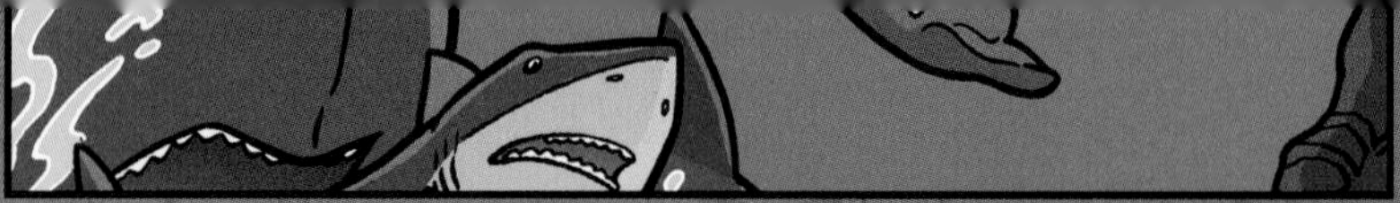

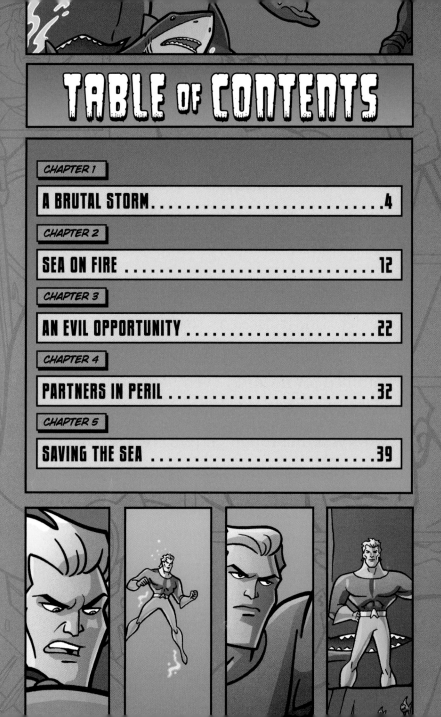

TABLE OF CONTENTS

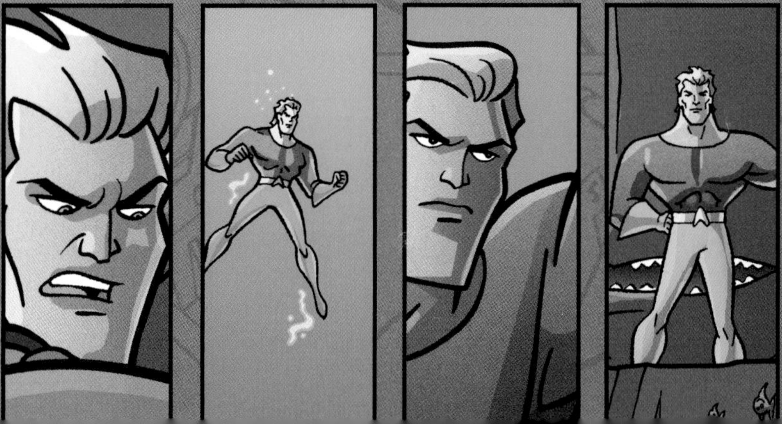

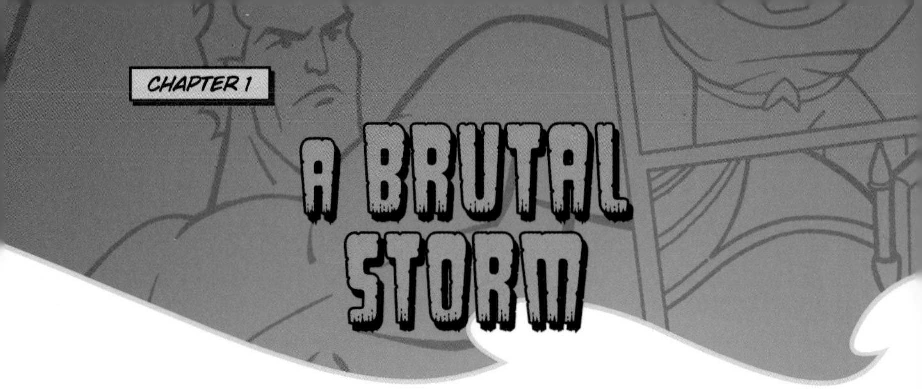

CHAPTER 1

A BRUTAL STORM

A wild storm raged in the Gulf of Mexico. Under the sea's steep waves, Aquaman followed the tempest and patrolled for hazards. Even below the surface, the water churned. Aquaman swam into the rough current. He used his superhuman strength to stay on course.

Along the coastline of Florida, the Sea King swooped over a reef of spiky staghorn and elkhorn coral. Brightly colored fish and eels hunkered in the coral beds. They hid in the jagged formations for protection.

"How are you holding up?" Aquaman asked a school of red snapper swimming into the current. They flashed their tails at him in panic.

"I know it's scary," the hero said. "Stay near the reef, and you should be fine."

A cast of blue crabs weathered the underwater turbulence by clinging to coral with their claws. Nearby, in an expanse of sea grasses, a group of silver tarpon huddled together. The tough plants sheltered the tarpon, helping them fight through the horrible conditions.

Satisfied that his kingdom would survive the storm, Aquaman headed closer to the surface. He scanned for the shadows of ships, but he didn't see any. The Coast Guard had contacted all sailors, urging them to come ashore before the storm hit.

Aquaman cruised along the shoreline. He kept watch from under the waves. He made sure all ships had followed the Coast Guard's orders. This storm was worse than anyone had expected. Someone trapped at sea would be in serious danger.

Then, echoing through the water, Aquaman heard the clang of a distant bell. *FWOOOSHHHHH!!* The super hero propelled himself toward the sound. *DING! DING! DING!* As the bell rang louder and faster, Aquaman spotted the rocking shadow of a small boat. Even from underwater, he could tell that the ship was having trouble staying upright.

Aquaman shot to the surface. As soon as his head rose above the water, he was smacked by the force of the storm.

Pounding rain pelted the hero's face. Wind whipped up 30-foot waves. Violent, dark clouds covered the sky in every direction, flashing with jags of lightning.

Thrusting upward on a rough wave, Aquaman saw the ship. It was a small shrimping boat. Two people clung to the deck. Another man held onto the ship's mast, frantically ringing a warning bell.

Aquaman surged closer to the boat. Then he leaped onboard.

"Aquaman!" a boy shouted. "Help us!"

The shrimp fishermen, including two men and the boy, were drenched and terrified. Aquaman sprinted to them as a monster wave loomed over the boat.

"Hold on to me!" Aquaman shouted.

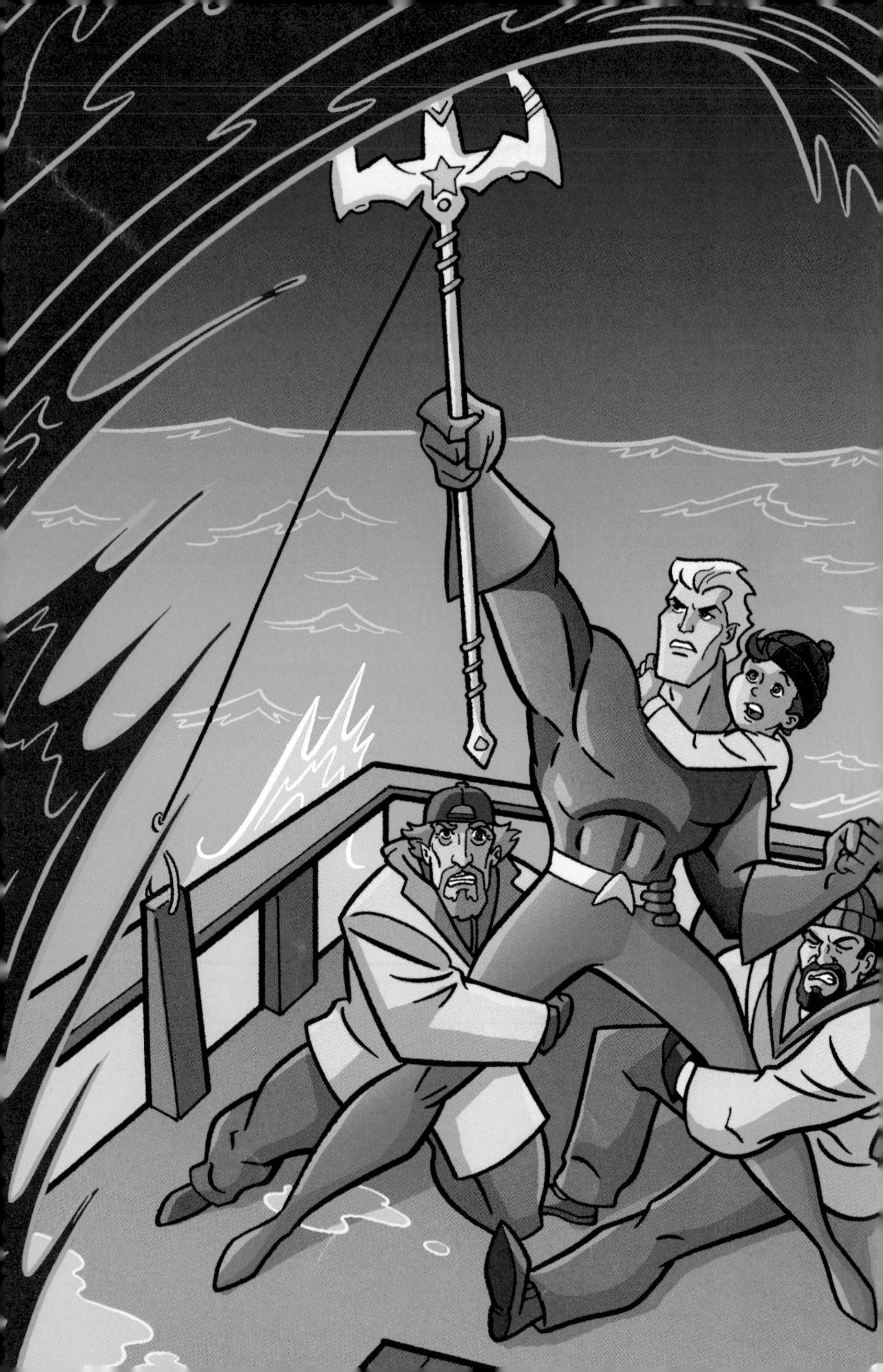

The two fishermen grabbed Aquaman by the legs. The boy clung to the hero's neck as the wave hit.

THWOOOOMMM!!

Aquaman leaped away from the sinking boat. He carried the three fishermen into the raging sea. He kicked hard in the water, managing to keep the heads of the two men and the boy above the surface.

The super hero knew he wouldn't be able to keep afloat long in such rough water. Concentrating, Aquaman sent out a command using his telepathic powers.

In moments, a bottlenose dolphin and a beluga whale popped their heads up into the storm. **SQUEAK! SQUEAK!** The dolphin squawked at Aquaman, and the beluga chirped.

"Thank you for coming quickly," Aquaman told the seagoing mammals.

The super hero quickly placed one of the men on the dolphin's back and the other on the beluga. The boy remained clinging to Aquaman's shoulders.

Swimming along the waves, the Sea King led the dolphin and the beluga closer to shore. They cruised into a protected bay where a Coast Guard base was located. The servicemen and women were surprised to see men riding a beluga and a dolphin.

"Thanks, Aquaman!" the boy shouted. "You saved all our lives!" He grinned at the dolphin and the beluga whale. "Thank you, too."

The dolphin and the beluga trilled happy sounds before swimming away.

As Aquaman turned to leave, a Coast Guard officer called out, "Aquaman, wait a moment!"

Aquaman looked up at the uniformed man standing on the dock. "Yes, officer?" asked the super hero.

The officer squatted down so he wouldn't have to shout. "We're getting alarming reports from the Sea Floor Explorer oil rig off the coast of Louisiana," he said. "Workers on the rig radioed for assistance, but since then we've lost contact. We're deploying helicopters and rescue ships. We were hoping you'd take a look, too."

"Yes, sir," Aquaman replied. "I'm on it."

SPLASH! The Sea King dived back under the waves and sped out to sea.

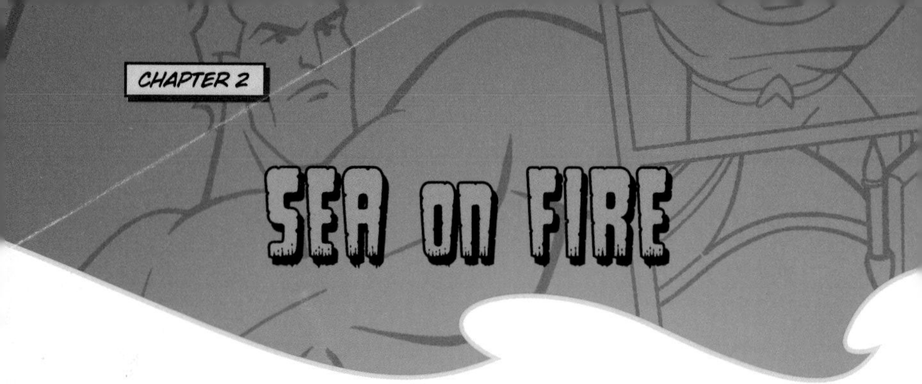

CHAPTER 2

SEA ON FIRE

ZWWWwOOOOMMMMM!

Aquaman shot across the Gulf at top speed. He rushed toward the oil rig off the Louisiana coast. Aquaman swam at mid-depth, low enough to avoid the worst of the choppy currents, but high enough that the water pressure didn't slow him.

As he cruised closer, Aquaman picked up troubled signals from the undersea life. Most humans didn't realize how often fish communicated with each other. The oceans of the world were an information network.

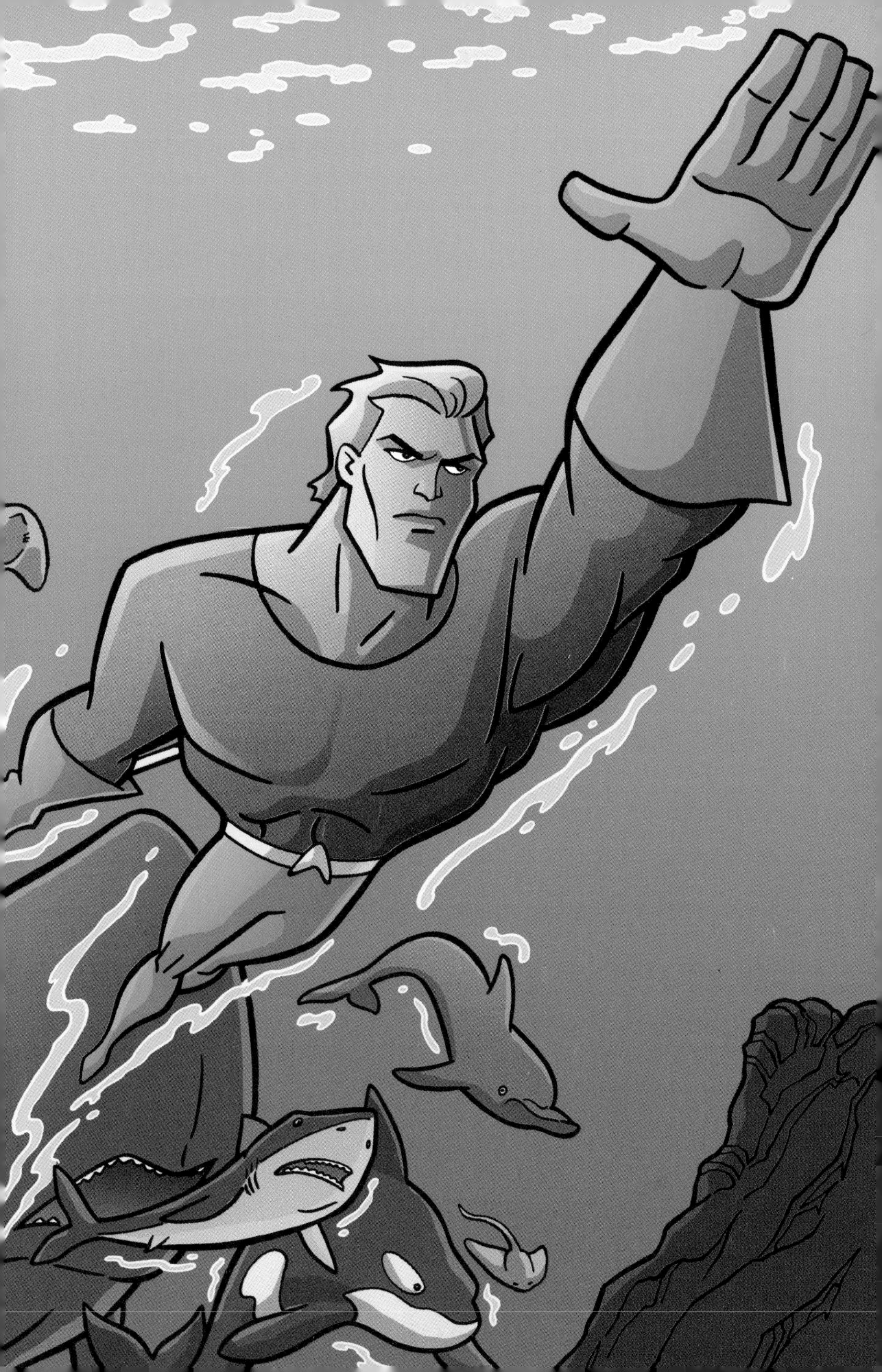

Fire! Aquaman overheard from a swarm of little squid. The tiny critters thought in images rather than words. *Fire on the water!*

A school of bluefin tuna had the same worry. As Aquaman zoomed past them, they warned, *You're going the wrong direction, Sire! This way to safety!*

Aquaman thanked them and swam on. Nearer to the rig, the undersea creatures were panicked and fleeing. Sea turtles and mako sharks rushed away from the area. The hero saw a pair of orcas and a pack of sturgeon hurrying in the opposite direction. Sea snakes swam away in fear.

Then Aquaman spotted the enormous pontoons that kept the oil rig afloat. He thrust up to the surface. With the storm dying down, the Sea King saw the disaster on the oil rig clearly.

The operating deck of the Sea Floor Explorer was ablaze. The oil rig wobbled in the rough water. Tongues of flame rose from the main derrick into the drizzly sky. Black smoke billowed off the platform.

Lifeboats filled with crew members were being lowered off the edges of the gigantic platform. Other workers who couldn't get to the lifeboats had to jump 80 feet into the churning water below.

As helicopters buzzed overhead, the Sea King dashed through the waves. He rushed toward the bobbing jumpers in their life jackets. He found a group of four men huddling together in the water, but the nearest rescue boat was too far away.

Aquaman sent out a telepathic command. In an instant, a sperm whale raised its blowhole up to the surface.

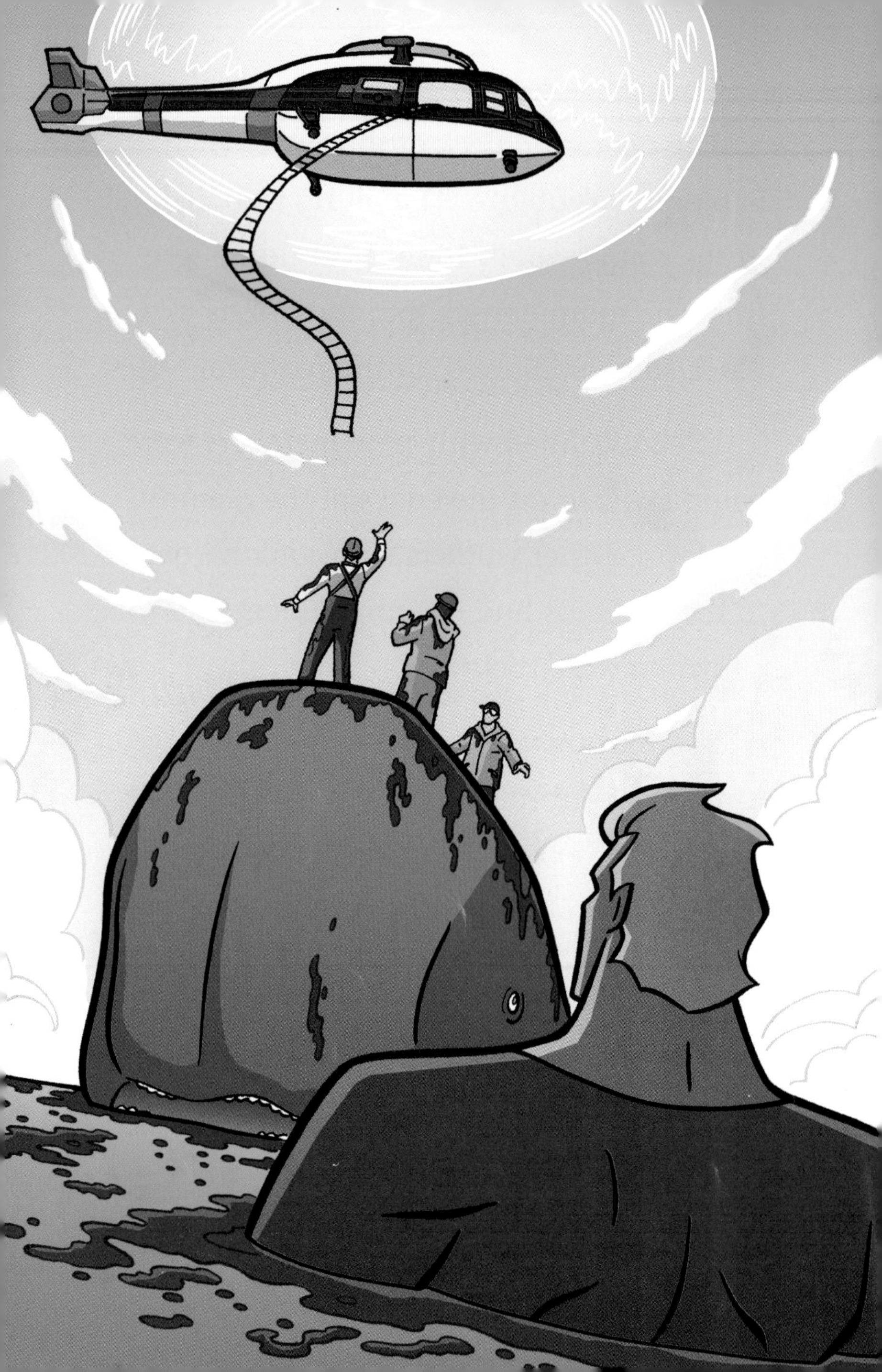

Aquaman pushed the men up onto the whale's broad back. The rescue helicopters could retrieve them from there.

"What happened?" Aquaman shouted to an older crew member.

The bearded man shook his head. "We're not sure," he gasped, clinging to the whale's back. "Maybe lightning hit the rig. Or maybe the storm smashed something in the piping. We'd all better get out of here, though. The tanks are full of crude oil. It's going to blow!"

Aquaman had to move fast. The super hero told the sperm whale to swim to a safe distance. Now he had to get everyone else out of the area, too!

First stop was the nearest Coast Guard rescue vessel. Aquaman leaped onboard.

The Sea King told the captain about the possible explosion. As the captain radioed the other ships and helicopters, Aquaman dived back into the water. He searched for any other workers.

Just as Aquaman decided everyone was safe, he spotted a bobbing head near one of the rig's giant supports. He surged over to the floating man, who was unconscious. Aquaman grabbed him in a rescue hold and dragged him to the nearest boat.

Suddenly, the tank exploded. A giant fireball rose up, expanding a hundred feet into the air. Even at a distance, the fiery blast hit Aquaman. He gave the lifeboat a shove away from the rig. Then he ducked under the water, cooling his scorched skin.

When he resurfaced, the fireball had died down, but the entire rig was ablaze. Fireboats sailed closer on all sides. They aimed jets of water at the platform.

BOOM! Another explosion rocked the rig. The screeching sound of tearing steel echoed over the water.

Aquaman watched as the platform cracked in the middle. It slowly split in half. The two giant burning pieces of the rig toppled to the sides.

SPLASH! With colossal clouds of steam and spouts of boiling water, the titanic pieces sank beneath the waves.

As the water settled, Aquaman could see a brown stain of crude oil. It spread in a burning pool across the Gulf's surface. The seawater was on fire.

Worst of all, the deepwater drill had still been connected when the rig exploded. Now the drill had snapped and shattered.

The wellhead was gashed open.

The ragged hole in the seabed was gushing a continuous geyser of poisonous crude oil into the Gulf of Mexico.

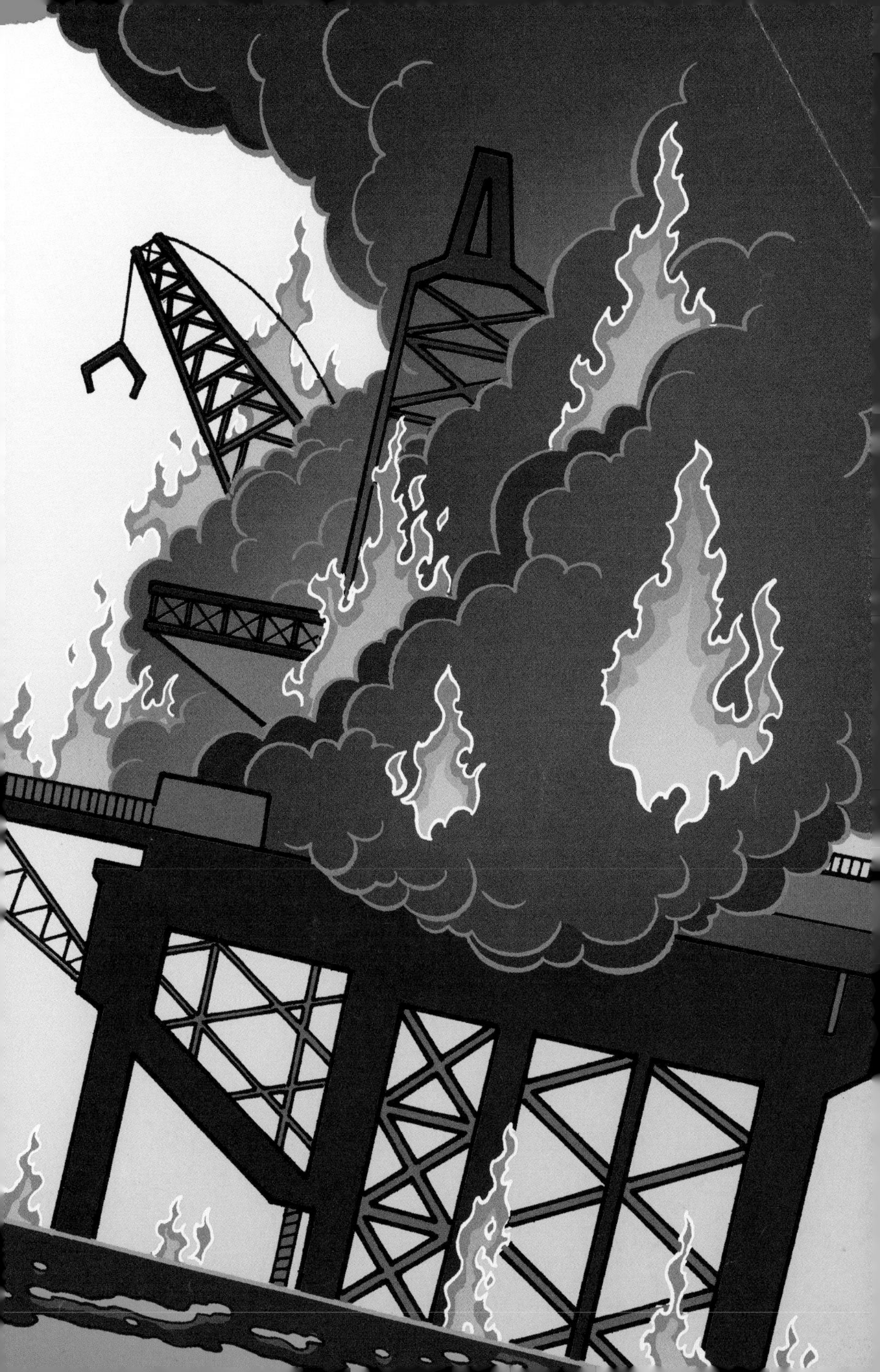

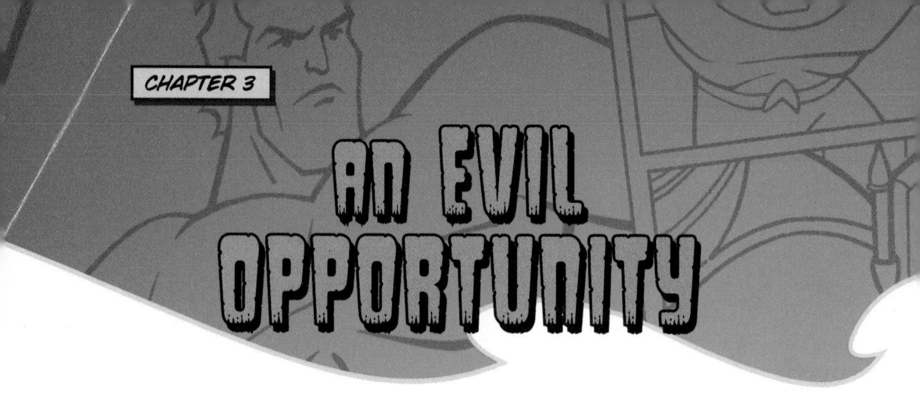

CHAPTER 3

AN EVIL OPPORTUNITY

Aquaman stared in shock at the fountain of oil flowing from the wellhead. Hundreds of gallons were gushing out every minute. If the leak wasn't stopped soon, the effects would be disastrous.

Aquaman's heart raced as he thought of all the terrible things that could happen to the Gulf of Mexico. He knew better than anyone that the Gulf was a delicate ecosystem. Hundreds of varieties of fish, plant life, sea mammals, and birds made their homes in the region.

Damage to Aquaman's undersea kingdom and its innocent inhabitants would be severe. Oil would ruin coral reefs and blacken the beaches. It could poison the beds of mussels and oysters, pollute the coastline, and contaminate the whole area.

Aquaman had to plug the leak fast!

Trying to think of a plan, Aquaman darted deeper and circled the fountain of oil. What he saw on the other side of the huge geyser stopped him cold in the water.

Sailing out of an oil plume was a small submarine. At first, Aquaman thought it might be a support vehicle investigating the leak. But when he recognized the submarine, Aquaman quickly slipped behind a piece of the sunken rig so he could observe unnoticed.

The submarine was shaped like a manta ray. Hidden behind the jagged piece of platform, Aquaman clenched his hands into fists. The sight of his archenemy's underwater vehicle filled him with anger.

"Black Manta!" Aquaman said to himself. "What is he doing here?" The villain showing up at an epic disaster could only be bad news. The super hero instantly suspected that Black Manta had somehow triggered the oil rig explosion.

But why would Black Manta pollute his own environment? the Sea King wondered.

In his own twisted way, Black Manta loved the ocean as much as Aquaman did, if only to steal its underwater treasures. Black Manta wanted to rule the seas, not destroy them. It made no sense. But then, the villain had always been crazy.

POP! The hatch of the submarine opened. Black Manta's protective helmet appeared. The villain swam a short distance toward the oil geyser. He dragged a tube that was connected to a tank on the submarine.

Black Manta stuck the end of the tube into the gushing oil. Then he pressed a button on a remote control. **CLICK!**

Aquaman narrowed his eyes angrily when the tube started suctioning up oil. **GURGLE!** The amount wasn't enough to slow the geyser. Black Manta was taking advantage of the disaster for his own gain.

Aquaman was sure that the villain had caused the fire. And for what? To collect a little crude oil? Shaking his head, Aquaman scolded himself for being shocked at the depths to which Black Manta would sink.

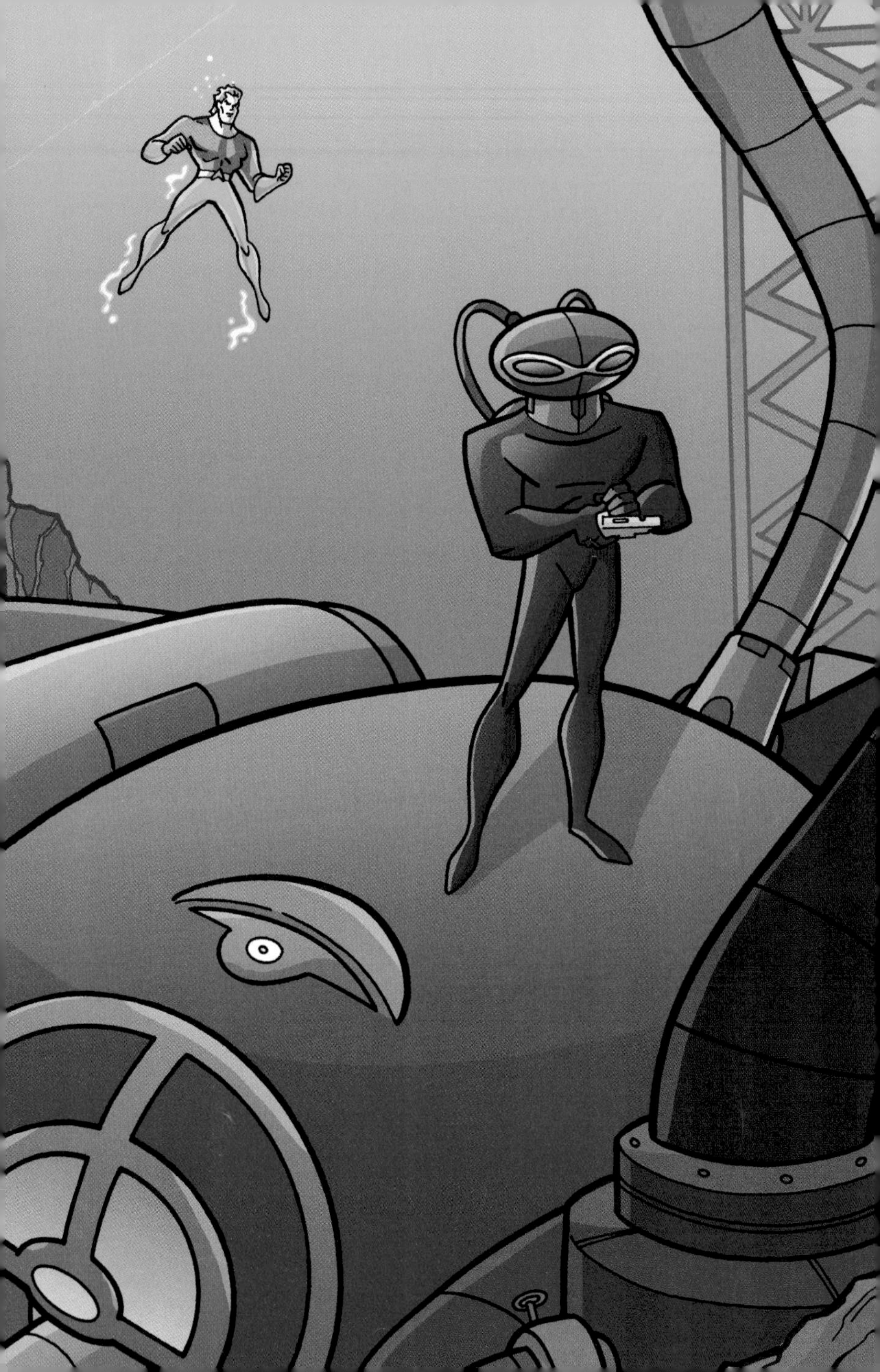

The super hero shouldn't have been surprised. After all, Black Manta had done many wicked things in the past. Now the villain had set off a disaster that could ruin the entire Gulf.

Fury overwhelmed Aquaman. He soared out from his hiding place. He rocketed at Black Manta like a torpedo. **ZOOOM!**

As soon as he was in swinging distance, Aquaman socked the villain in his helmet with his fist. **THWACK!**

Black Manta staggered, but he quickly recovered. He shot laser blasts at Aquaman from the eyes of his helmet.

BWEEOOOM! BWEEOOOM! Aquaman somersaulted to avoid the deadly beams. He circled around and tackled Black Manta, knocking him to the sea floor.

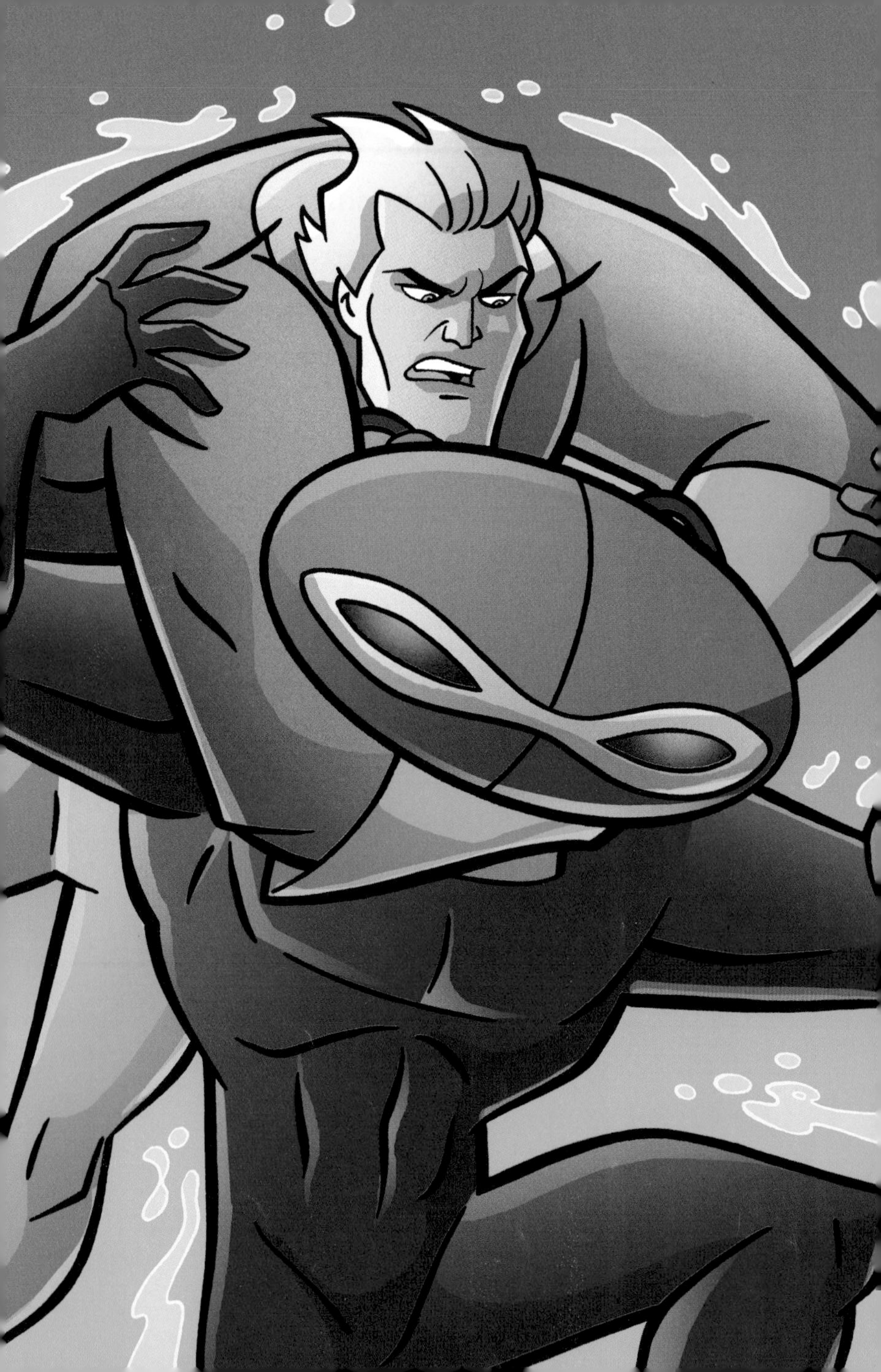

With a wild kick, Black Manta freed himself. The villain tried to hit Aquaman again with his lasers. Aquaman slipped to the side, and the lasers ignited a plume of oil. Black Manta had to leap away to avoid the burst of flame, but the fire fizzled quickly in the water.

While Black Manta was off balance, Aquaman jetted behind him. He grabbed the villain in a tight grip around his neck.

"Why?" Aquaman demanded. "Why would you destroy an entire oil rig to fill your submarine's tank?"

Black Manta struggled in Aquaman's hold. "I did nothing of the sort!" he said in a deep, robotic voice. "I didn't blow up the rig, but I couldn't pass up some black gold. I saw an opportunity for free oil . . . and took advantage of it."

Thinking Black Manta was lying, Aquaman tightened his grip on the villain's neck.

When Black Manta didn't struggle, the Sea King calmed down. The villain's explanation made sense. Black Manta had nothing to gain from polluting the Gulf. Still, Aquaman could see how a low-life scavenger like Black Manta couldn't resist the chance to benefit from such a catastrophe.

Lost in thought, Aquaman was surprised when Black Manta savagely elbowed him in the stomach. **WHAM!** The villain broke free.

 Black Manta darted a few feet away. He whirled around, preparing to blast Aquaman with his lasers.

His stomach aching, Aquaman stared at Black Manta. "You fool!" the hero shouted at the villain. "If this leak isn't stopped, neither of us will win. Everything we treasure in the ocean will be gone for good!"

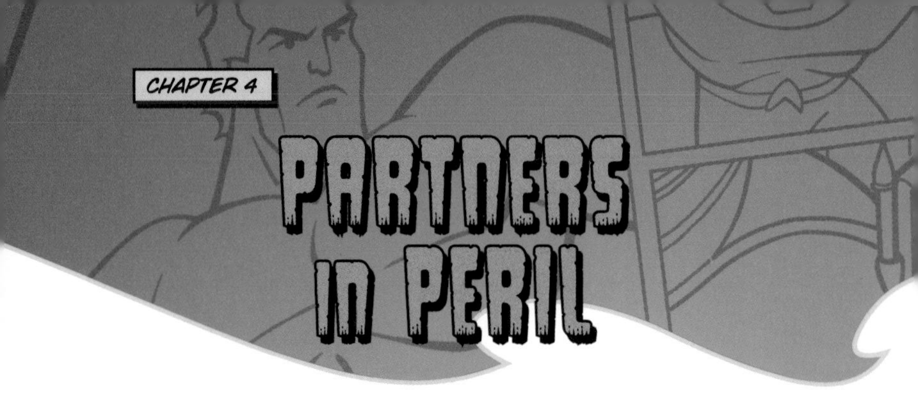

CHAPTER 4

PARTNERS IN PERIL

For a long moment, Black Manta didn't move. He didn't fire his lasers.

Aquaman waited, floating in the water. Part of him insisted that he protect himself, or attack his archenemy. But Aquaman had bigger concerns on his mind. To stop the destruction of his environment, the hero needed all the help he could get.

"You may have a point," Black Manta said finally. He nodded his helmet. "I have no wish to rule over a ruined wasteland."

"I suggest a temporary truce," replied Aquaman. "For the good of the sea."

"Yes," said Black Manta. "*Temporary.*"

Aquaman turned around. He wanted to show that he temporarily trusted Black Manta as he surveyed the disaster area. The sea grasses around the geyser were smashed by rubble. Oyster and mussel beds had been crushed by debris. Chunks of melted metal littered the seafloor, which blocked easy access to the wellhead.

"First, we need to clean up," Aquaman said. "We can't stop the leak if we can't get to it."

Black Manta started dragging pieces of rubble away with his submarine. Aquaman called the dolphins. He asked sharks, whales, and turtles to help as well.

Aquaman apologized for calling the creatures back to the toxic site, but they were happy to help. The hero used all his super-strength to move debris into a pile away from the leak. He wouldn't ask the creatures to do anything he wouldn't do himself.

While the Sea King and his creatures were busy, scientists and disaster aid workers joined the cleanup effort. The company that had owned Sea Floor Explorer was being held responsible for the damage. They were paying for all the workers and equipment.

Cleaning up the area took days. Meanwhile, more and more oil gushed into the Gulf. Experts tried shutting off emergency valves in the wellhead, but they'd all been too damaged.

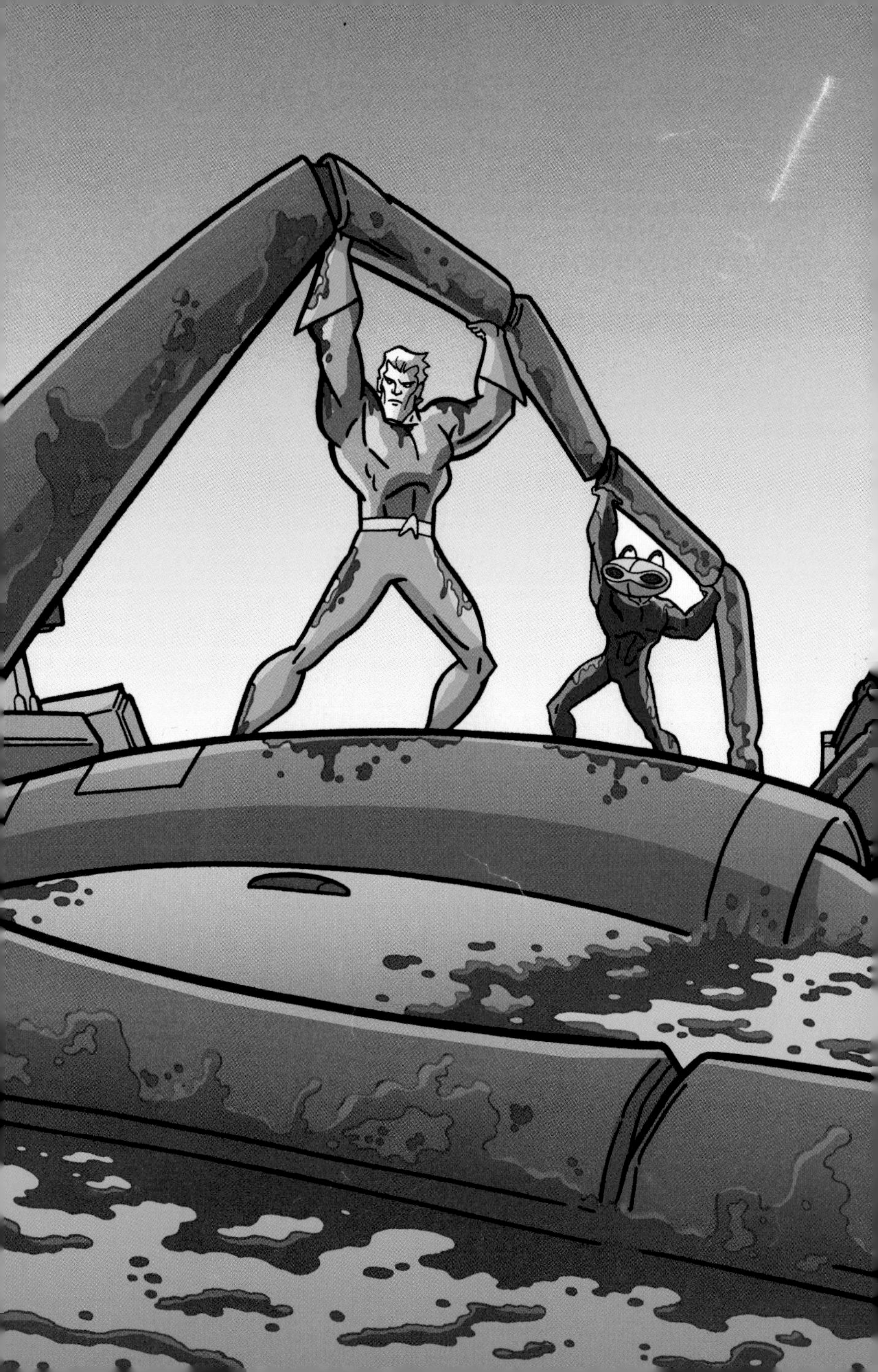

When space had been cleared around the leak, workers lowered an enormous hose to suction oil up to a tanker ship. They captured some oil, but barely a fraction of what was being released.

Next, scientists suggested filling in the hole with debris from the rig. Aquaman, his undersea friends, and Black Manta helped drag smaller pieces of rubble to dump into the hole. The pressure of the surging oil was too strong. Nothing could block it.

The underwater environment grew more poisonous with each passing day. Aquaman lost track of how long he'd been working. He wouldn't give up.

On the surface, the oil slick oozed along the coast and spread toward the open ocean. Aquaman swore he would work until he dropped to save his watery realm.

Aquaman was surprised by how tirelessly Black Manta also labored. He had thought that the villain cared about nothing, but that wasn't true. His archenemy cared about the ocean, if nothing else.

One day, Aquaman met with the scientists on their ship. The experts were arguing about what to try next.

Aquaman had trouble listening. He kept staring glumly out at the brown stain on the water stretching into the distance.

Emergency workers had set up containment booms. These floating fences were supposed to help corral the oil, but they were only partially effective. There was not much they could do to keep millions of gallons of crude oil from oozing in every direction.

"We need to cap the leak," said the lead scientist in charge. "But we don't have anything heavy or big enough to withstand the oil pressure. Even if we did, we couldn't lift it into place. We don't have any cranes that will work that deep."

Aquaman snapped to attention. "A cap?" he asked. "Would a natural rock work if it was big enough?"

"I suppose," the scientist replied. "It would have to be a mighty big boulder, though! And how would we maneuver it into place?"

"I think I know just the thing," Aquaman said. "Leave it to Black Manta and me."

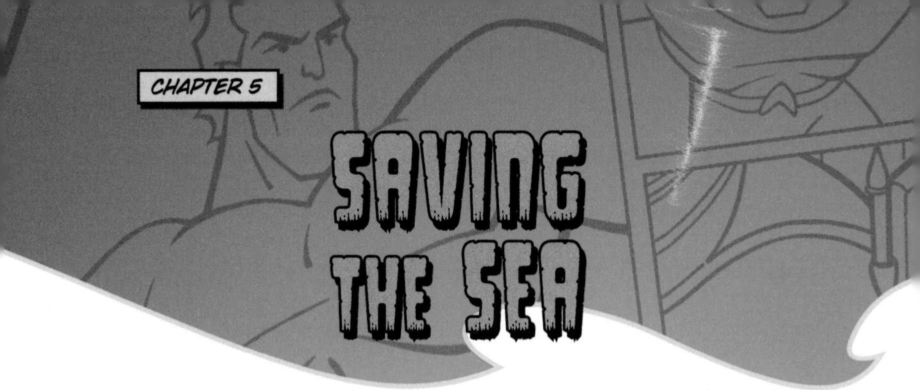

CHAPTER 5

SAVING THE SEA

Aquaman dived back to the depths, relieved that he had a plan, no matter how difficult it would be. He found Black Manta and told his enemy what he was thinking.

The wide coastal shelf around the leak was made up of softer, flat, sedimentary rock that wouldn't work. They would have to go farther into the Gulf, to the shelf edge, to find a useful boulder.

Aquaman telepathically asked his marine friends to search as well.

Both Black Manta and Aquaman hunted along the edge of the coastal shelf. After days of searching, they finally reached the rim of Green Canyon. There, a serpent-like oarfish told Aquaman about a promising find.

A huge chunk of the shelf had recently broken off from the top of the canyon. The flat hunk of sedimentary rock had crashed down at an angle on a lower ledge.

Aquaman and Black Manta rushed to investigate. They found the slab of rock exactly as the oarfish had described. Now they had to somehow lift it up the canyon wall and carry it to the leak site.

Quickly, Aquaman came up with a plan. He would need a lot of help to carry it out. Every creature would play a part.

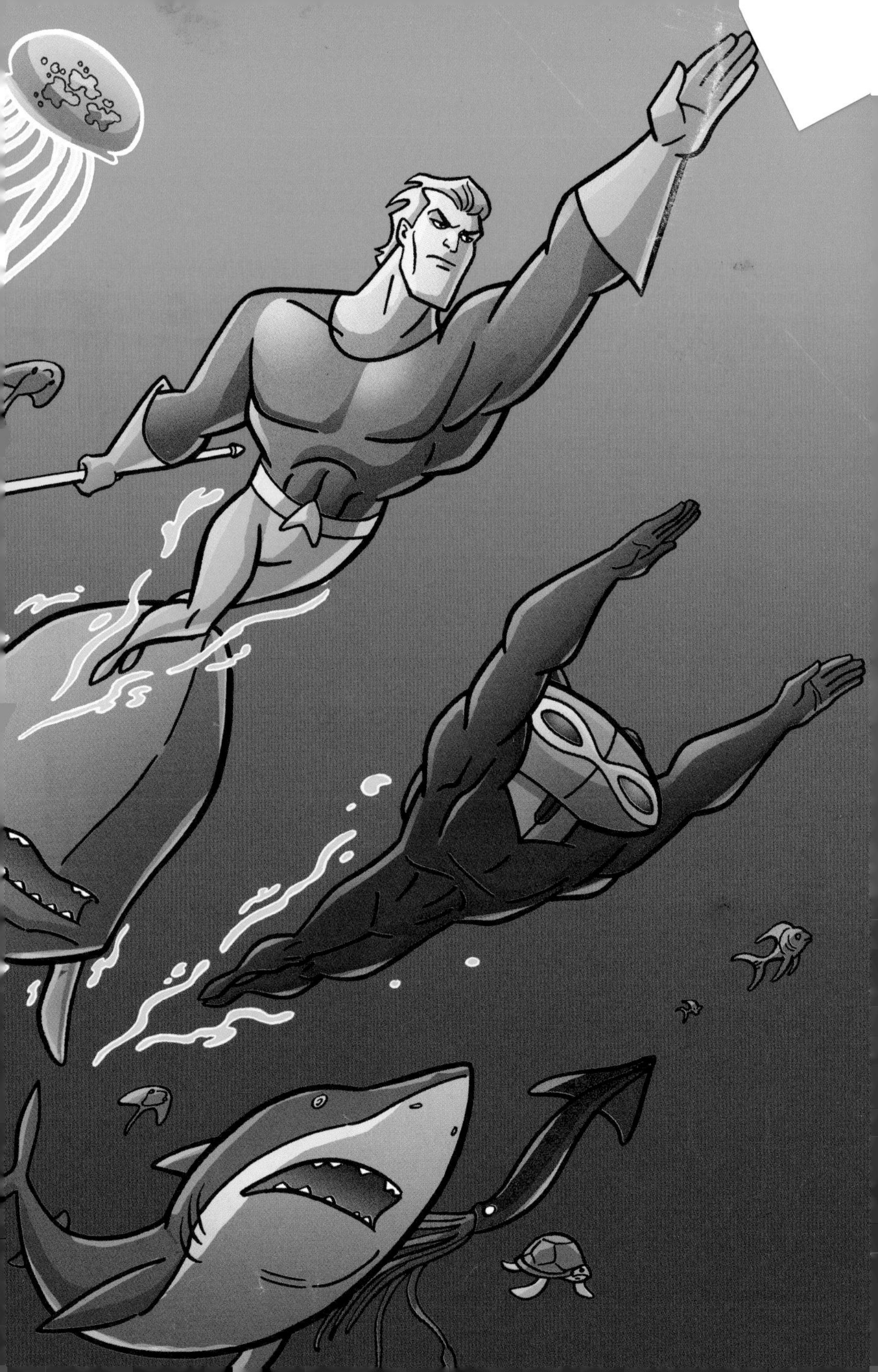

The Sea King sent out a telepathic signal, calling all creatures to help.

In the next few hours, an incredible variety of creatures answered Aquaman's request. Fish of all kinds and sizes came to help, including tuna, shad, groupers, mahi mahi, tarpon, sturgeon, sawfish, marlins, and tiny topminnows. Stingrays showed up with moray eels. Hundreds of nurse sharks, tiger sharks, dusky sharks, and hammerheads arrived as well.

They were joined by five different types of sea turtles and multiple species of dolphin. Blue whales, sperm whales, and humpback whales whistled mournfully at the edges of the gathering. Even cranky crustaceans showed up to help.

Creatures that usually ate each other swam side by side to save their world.

Aquaman directed the smaller and medium-sized creatures into the space beneath the tilted rock. He instructed the others to wait below the shelf. Then the super hero swam under the rock. Black Manta's submarine moved into position with the waiting creatures outside, including most of the larger sea animals.

All together, the creatures under the massive slab heaved against the topmost part of the rock. It was a group effort the likes of which Aquaman had never witnessed before. The hero pushed as hard as he could, along with all the living things around him.

Slowly, the top of the slab pulled free from the shelf wall. When it was fully upright, the boulder teetered, and then toppled down off the edge of the shelf.

Black Manta's submarine and the larger sea animals caught the heavy slab. Aquaman led the rest of the sea creatures under the slab, too. They helped bear the enormous weight of the rock.

With incredible effort, they all carried the slab to the top of the canyon. Then they slowly lugged it toward the leak.

The task took hours of struggle. Some creatures had to stop from exhaustion, but their places were quickly taken by others.

Finally, they reached the geyser of oil. Aquaman directed his loyal sea dwellers to move the slab into place. The creatures let the rock slide off their backs. Black Manta's submarine zipped out from under the rock.

The slab crashed onto the leak.

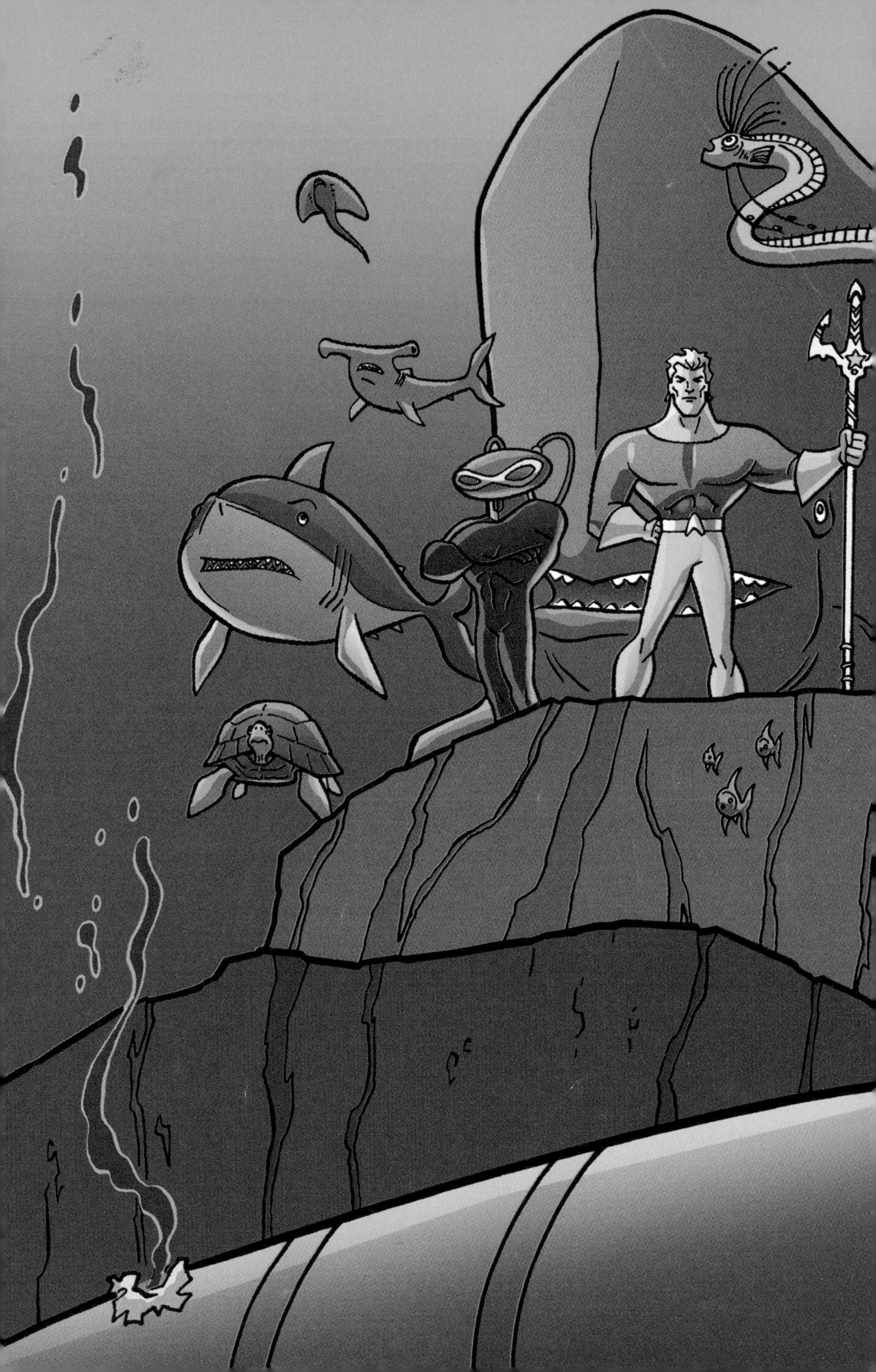

After a tremendous impact, the slab settled into the soft seabed. It smothered the leak, cutting it off completely.

They had covered the geyser like the lid of a tomb. The leak was capped.

Aquaman felt like celebrating, but he looked around at all the oil oozing through the water and stopped himself. The spill still spread across the water's surface. No more oil would spill from this leak, but dreadful damage had been done already.

Black Manta stuck his helmeted head out of his submarine.

"Our truce has come to an end," he said. "Don't expect me to show you any mercy when we meet again."

"And expect none from me," Aquaman replied.

Black Manta ducked into his submarine and cruised away, disappearing in the depths of the Gulf. Despite their surprising truce, Aquaman was not sorry to see his archenemy go.

Now Aquaman faced the biggest sea cleanup in history. He'd used the help of the ocean's biggest creatures to stop the leak. Aquaman knew a way to hurry the cleanup of the oil, using the aid of the sea's smallest inhabitants.

He called out for microbes. Many species of microorganisms fed off petroleum. They could devour some of the oil. Unfortunately, the microbes would leave many of the worst poisons behind, affecting the water's oxygen levels and causing devastation to the food chain. It might take years, or even decades, for the Gulf to recover.

With a huge sigh, Aquaman addressed all the sea creatures around him. "My loyal subjects," he told them, "in this time of our greatest tragedy, some of you must stay and help. Some of you must escape to places where you can be safe. But ultimately, we must trust the land dwellers to clean up our home."

Aquaman gazed at the sickly brown plumes of oil floating around the water. The toxins soiled the sea grasses, fouled the coral reefs, and suffocated the ecosystem.

"One day," he swore, "our oceans will be restored to their natural glory!"

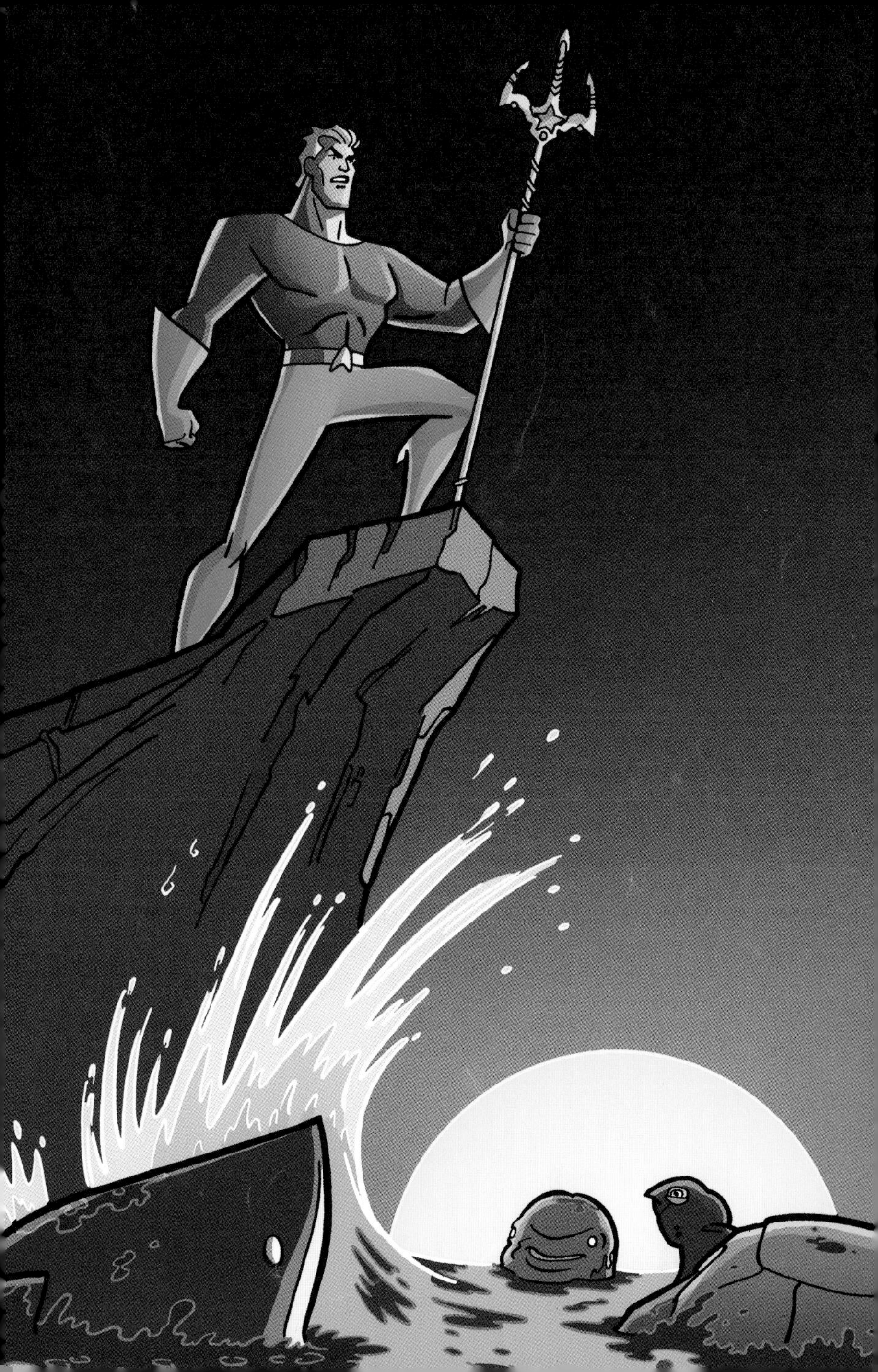

BLACK MANTA

REAL NAME: Unknown

OCCUPATION: Assassin

HEIGHT: 6' 4" **WEIGHT:** 250 lbs.

EYES: Brown   **HAIR:** Brown

POWERS/ABILITIES:
Possesses above-average strength; quickly masters new equipment; fueled by extreme rage.

BIOGRAPHY

Before Black Manta became a super-villain, he was a young boy with a severe illness. The world above sea level made his skin crawl. His only comfort . . . water. Scientists tried hundreds of experiments to reverse the condition, but the treatments only filled the child with anger. Then one day, the boy witnessed Aquaman on television and became inspired. He designed a high-tech, submersible costume and took the name Black Manta. Soon, this deepwater devil unleashed his rage upon the sea!

Black Manta modeled his high-tech uniform after real-life sea creatures called manta rays. The fully submersible uniform allows the super-villain to breathe underwater. The uniform is also equipped with a variety of gadgetry, including jet boots, miniature torpedoes, wrist gauntlets, and energy beams.

Although his uniform allows Black Manta to swim at super-speed, the villain often travels from place to place in a manta-ray shaped submarine. This sub carries deadly torpedoes and has a reinforced hull that is nearly indestructible.

Black Manta has two goals — destroy Aquaman and rule the seas. The villain will stop at nothing to achieve these evil objectives. During one of his many attacks, Black Manta killed Aquaman's son, Arthur Curry, Jr. However, this tragic event didn't stop the Sea King's fight against evil. Ever since, he has worked even harder to defend the ocean, protect its creatures, and shut down Black Manta once and for all.

BIOGRAPHIES

J.E. Bright has had more than 50 novels, novelizations, and non-fiction books published for children and young adults. He is a full-time freelance writer, living in a tiny apartment in the SoHo neighborhood of Manhattan with his good, fat cat, Gladys, and his evil cat, Mabel, who is getting fatter.

Dan Schoening was born in Victoria, B.C., Canada. From an early age, Dan has had a passion for animation and comic books. Currently, Dan does freelance work in the animation and game industry and spends a lot of time with his lovely little daughter, Paige.

Mike DeCarlo is a longtime contributor of comic art whose range extends from Batman and Iron Man to Bugs Bunny and Scooby-Doo. He resides in Connecticut with his wife and four children.

Lee Loughridge has been working in comics for more than fifteen years. He currently lives in sunny California in a tent on the beach.

GLOSSARY

booms (BOOMZ)— temporary floating barriers used to contain an oil spill

contaminate (kuhn-TAM-uh-nayt)—make dirty or unfit for use

derrick (DER-ik)—a tall framework that holds the machines used to drill oil wells

devour (di-VOUR)—to eat something quickly and hungrily

ecosystem (EE-koh-siss-tuhm)—a community of animals and plants interacting with their environment

sedimentary (sed-uh-MEN-tuh-ree)—rock formed by layers of sediment in the ground that has been pressed together

telepathic (teh-luh-PATH-ik)—communicating from one mind to another without speaking

tempest (TEM-pist)—a violent storm

turbulence (TUR-byuh-lunts)—wild or irregular motions, such as up-and-down currents in the wind or water

DISCUSSION QUESTIONS

1. Why did Aquaman need Black Manta's help? Could the super hero have stopped the oil spill without his enemy? Explain your answers.

2. Oil spills impact people all over the world. Discuss at least two ways oil spills can affect people who don't live near the ocean.

3. Discuss the pros and cons of drilling for oil in the ocean. What are some of the benefits? What are some of the drawbacks?

WRITING PROMPTS

1. Newspapers and websites are great places to find story ideas. Read an article about a current event. Then, use the people, places, and facts of that report to write a fictional short story.

2. Write another Aquaman adventure! Will he stop another disaster? Will he face off against a different underwater enemy? You decide.

3. Aquaman protects the seas. Create a super hero that protects a different part of Earth. Give your hero a name, and write a story about him or her.

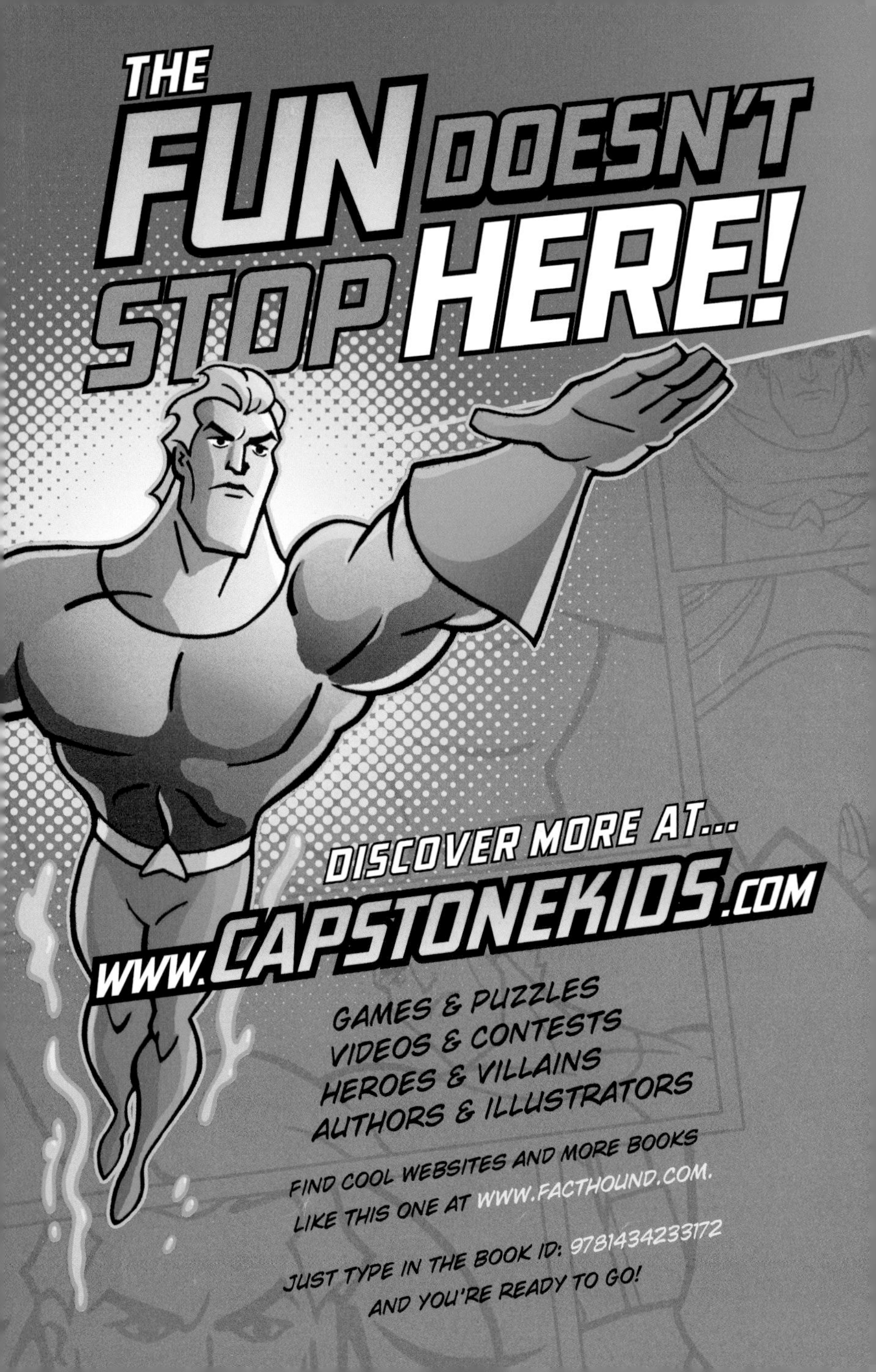
THE FUN DOESN'T STOP HERE!
DISCOVER MORE AT...
WWW.CAPSTONEKIDS.COM
GAMES & PUZZLES
VIDEOS & CONTESTS
HEROES & VILLAINS
AUTHORS & ILLUSTRATORS
FIND COOL WEBSITES AND MORE BOOKS
LIKE THIS ONE AT WWW.FACTHOUND.COM.
JUST TYPE IN THE BOOK ID: 9781434233172
AND YOU'RE READY TO GO!

MORE SUPER DC HEROES ADVENTURES!

SUPERMAN

BATMAN

WONDER WOMAN

GREEN LANTERN

THE FLASH

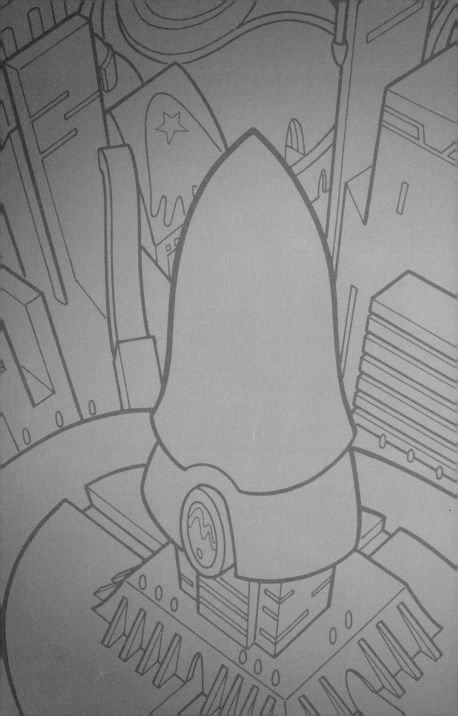

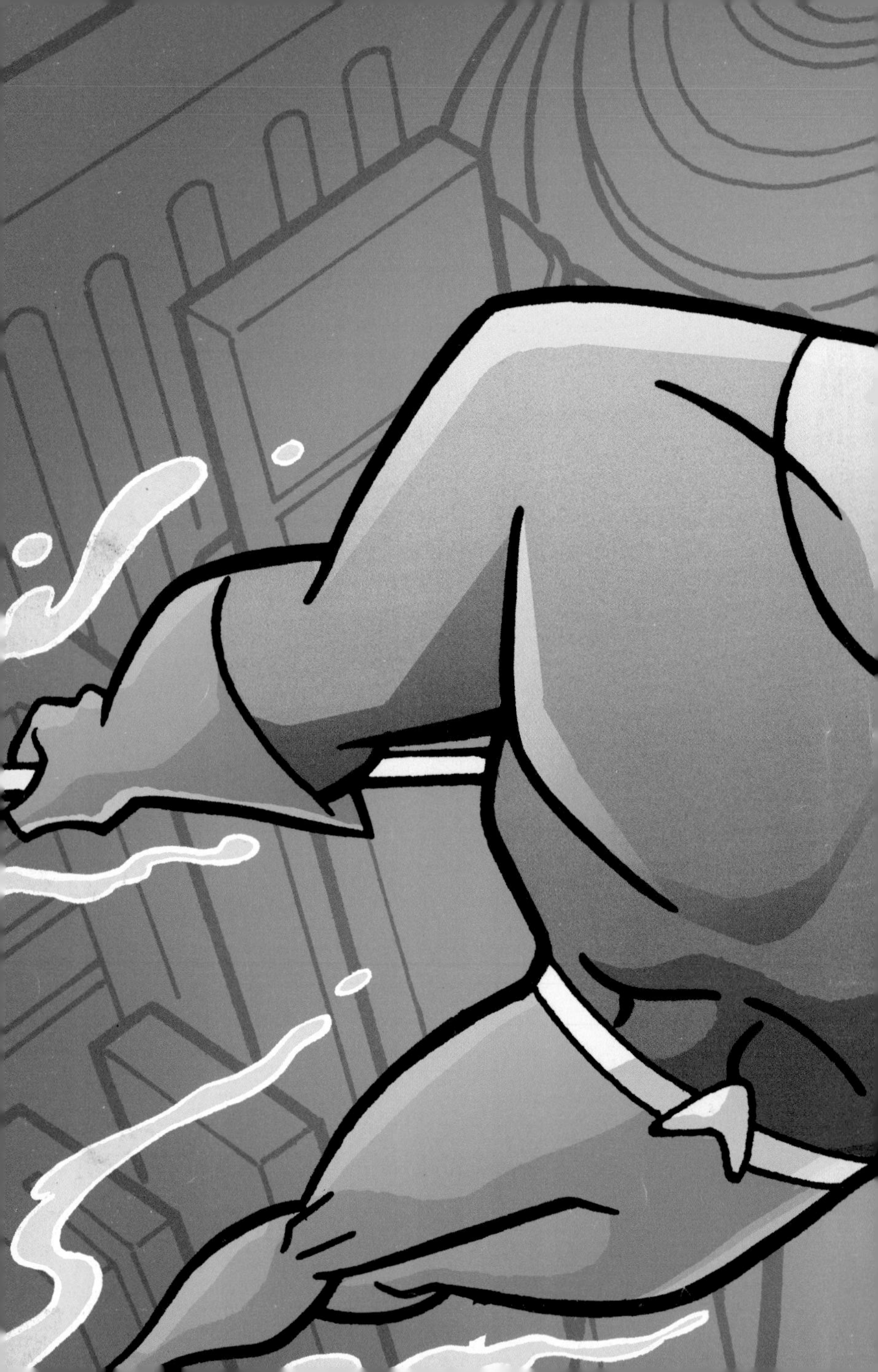